MW00874499

CAMERON THE CAMERA

Written By:
Nathan Fleischer
Caroline Hoffman

Illustrations By:
Nathan Fleischer

Copyright © 2021 Nathan Fleischer
All rights reserved.

No part of this publication may be reproduced, stored in a retrieval system, or transmitted in any form or by any means, electronic, mechanical, photocopying, recording (including but not limited to storytime videos), or otherwise without written permission from the publisher. For information regarding permission, write to Nathan Fleische

Published in Chicago, IL

Library of Congress Control Number: 2021914358

ISBN:
978-1-7369785-0-4 Paperback
978-1-7369785-1-1 Ebook
978-1-7369785-2-8 Hardcover

Dear Reader,

Even if your gifts look different from someone else's, remember to keep using them.

-N

Cameron the camera was the favorite toy,
Taking photos of the others was such a joy.

Her lens was clean and her flash was bright,
She could take pictures all day and all night.

Carly was her owner, and Cameron felt her best,

When Carly took Cameron and started to press.

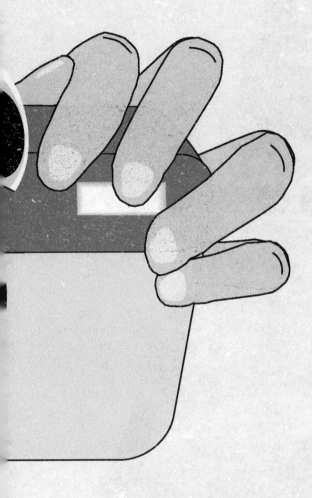

Finally, when she heard her own button click,

That's when she knew she took the perfect pic.

Cameron took photos of the crayons and toy cars
The figurines, the dolls, and the drawings of Mars
The horses, the elephants, the stuffed kangaroos
The puzzles, the skates and worn ballet shoes.

Carly came home with a smile on her face.
She was carrying something new, a rose-colored case.

COME QUICK!!

She said "come quick!" She was very excited.
The photographs were ready - everyone was delighted.

Cameron and the other toys gathered around,
All the toys erupted in joyous sound.

But Cameron's smile flipped upside down,

When no photos of Cameron were to be found.

Cameron would never be in her pictures,
She walked away thinking nothing could fix her.

Some other toys noticed this shift in her mood,
To cheer her up, the easy bake oven whipped up some food.

The barbies offered a ride in their Corvette,

Hot beverages from the teacups, the whole ten piece set!

The picture books said they could read her to sleep,

The sheep would be orchestrated by Little Bo Peep

Although Cameron thought their gestures were kind

She felt her flash dim, it no longer shined

The other toys were sad and feeling so blue

All of a sudden, the crayons knew just what to do

We have an idea!

The crayons went and got Carly's picture book,

They said, "we have an idea come quick, come look!"

Carly heard the crayons make a bustling sound,

They had a great plan, if Carly allowed.

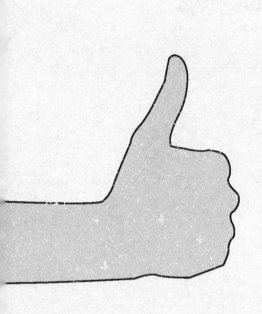

"We should come together, please use us to draw,

A picture of all of us to leave Cameron in awe."

"Let's add highlights and shadows, and color the most!

It won't be a photograph but it will come close."

When it was ready, they prepared for the surprise.

They called over Cameron, and covered her eyes.

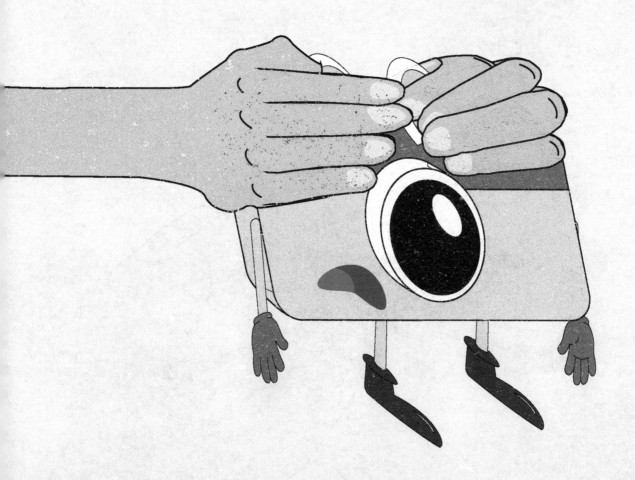

They counted to three and showed her together.

Cameron and the toys, finally framed forever.

In Cameron's happiness and excitement she started to laugh

She thought to herself "I should take a photograph!"

She still wanted to capture this moment and knew,

That this is what Cameron was still meant to do.

It doesn't matter if you're always in the frame

It matters what you do, how you feel, and what you say

To be kind, to have fun, and to often say please

For she'd always be loved by those who said "CHEESE!"

THE

END

CPSIA information can be obtained
at www.ICGtesting.com
Printed in the USA
BVHW010722010921
615417BV00042B/372

9 781736 978528